To my beloved girls, Arrietty, Niamh,
Phoebe and Primrose,
May you grow up in a wild and
wonderful world.

Emma
x y

We support
REWiLDiNG
BRiTAiN

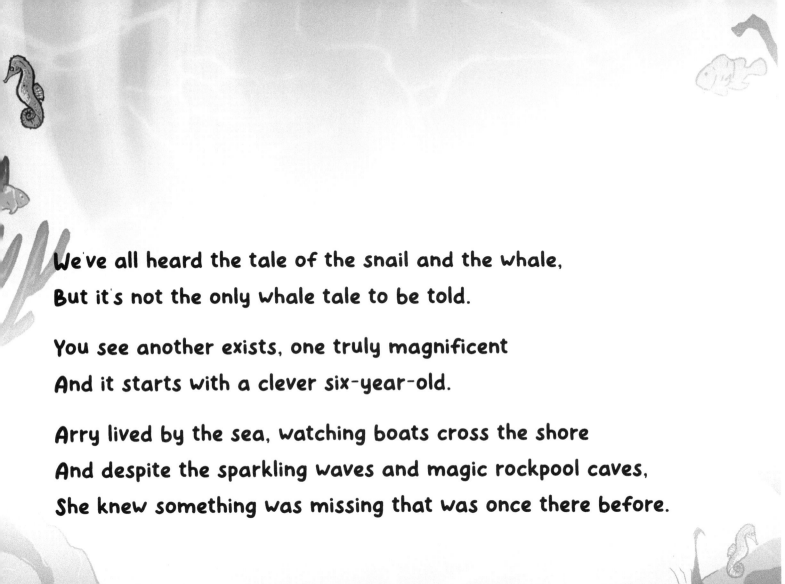

We've all heard the tale of the snail and the whale,
But it's not the only whale tale to be told.

You see another exists, one truly magnificent
And it starts with a clever six-year-old.

Arry lived by the sea, watching boats cross the shore
And despite the sparkling waves and magic rockpool caves,
She knew something was missing that was once there before.

A giant of a creature with a mighty forehead feature
And a mouth big enough to eat ginormous waves.

She stared at her grandma's photos bemused and bewildered
And wished the once wild ocean wasn't now so cluttered.

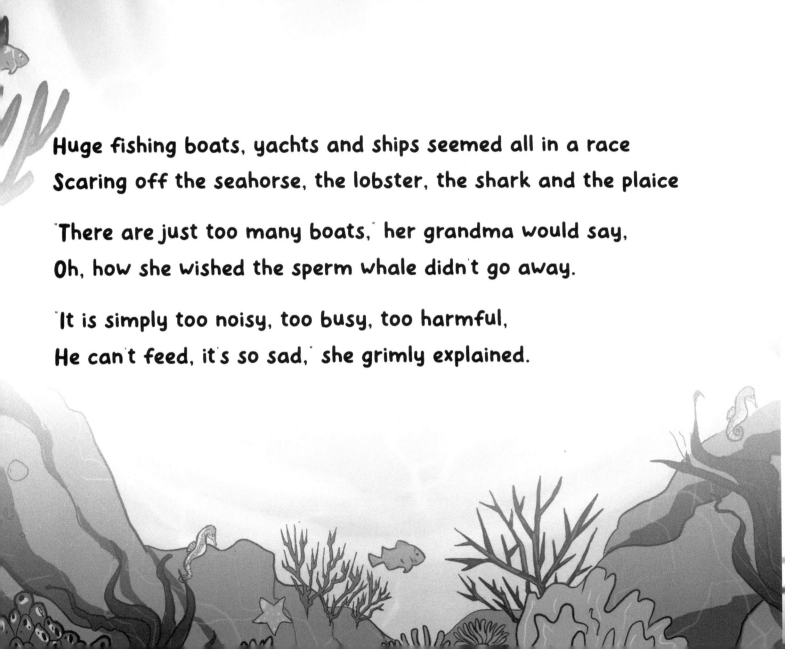

Huge fishing boats, yachts and ships seemed all in a race
Scaring off the seahorse, the lobster, the shark and the plaice

"There are just too many boats," her grandma would say,
Oh, how she wished the sperm whale didn't go away.

"It is simply too noisy, too busy, too harmful,
He can't feed, it's so sad," she grimly explained.

Arry knew this wasn't right and wanted something done,
one million sperm whales once lived where soon there could be none.

She fetched pen and paper and wrote with all her heart,
She sent a letter to her Prime Minister and created whale art.

She told friends and family and presented at school,
Everybody agreed bringing back whales would be cool.

"Just imagine it," Arry beamed, her arms wide in the air
"A creature bigger than buses who wears invisible hair!"

She captivated everyone, making people stop and think,
How empty our oceans had become, the whale on the brink.

They took their signs to the streets and knocked on peoples' doors
'Help us save the sperm whale, help us protect our ocean floor'.

Soon others joined her mission to inspire change,
They campaigned to rewild their sea, and everyone engaged.

A community united, their signs and protests full of hope,
Under all the pressure, the government could not cope.

Things suddenly changed, it was magical to see,
A 'Highly Protected Marine Zone' was declared, and the ocean was set free.

Project restoration started straight-away,
Divers replanted the seagrass and once more they swayed.

Shy seahorse returned hiding among the kelp
Where colourful puffins dived, all thanks to Arry's help.

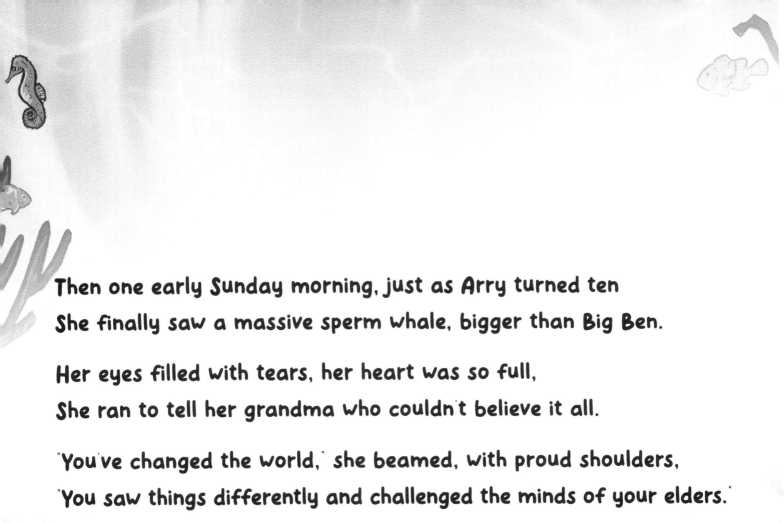

Then one early Sunday morning, just as Arry turned ten
She finally saw a massive sperm whale, bigger than Big Ben.

Her eyes filled with tears, her heart was so full,
She ran to tell her grandma who couldn't believe it all.

"You've changed the world," she beamed, with proud shoulders,
"You saw things differently and challenged the minds of your elders."

You see, Arry had a special gift that made our planet better,
It all started with being caring and brave enough to write a letter

And all those things inside her, also live in you
Arry hopes you'll grow up doing something magical for
our planet too.

Let's learn about rewilding

Rewilding is a special way of helping nature take care of itself.

We do this by letting nature return to its natural state. We remove things that might be harming the environment and restore habitats and remove barriers.

When we let trees grow tall, rivers flow freely, and animals have lots of space to move around, something amazing happens. It creates a healthy and balanced ecosystem! That means animals, plants, and insects can all live together and help each other survive. This happens not just on land, but also in the oceans and seas.

Sometimes, we notice that some animals have disappeared from certain places. That's not good because those animals play an important role in keeping everything in balance. So, in rewilding, we try to bring back those missing animals to their homes. We want them to be where they belong and do the important jobs they're meant to do.

Rewilding helps people too. When nature is happy and healthy, it gives us clean air to breathe, safe water to drink and lots of delicious food. Plus, we get to enjoy the beauty of nature all around us.

By rewilding nature, we're also taking care of ourselves. Isn't that amazing?

Milton Keynes UK
Ingram Content Group UK Ltd.
UKHW050511131023
430478UK00009B/97